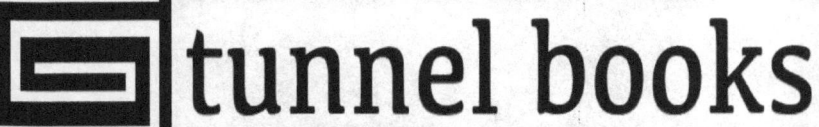

tunnel books

THE FROG
RUY BURGOS-LOVECE

TRANSLATED FROM SPANISH
BY THE AUTHOR

TUNNEL BOOKS
PITTSBURGH
2015

THE FROG
© Ruy Burgos-Lovece
Translation © Ruy Burgos-Lovece
©Editorial Paroxismo
Tunnel Books Collection

ISBN
0692411631

www.editorial-paroxismo.com

Cover, design, and composition by FLC

Printed in the United States of America

ACTUALLY, the greatest advantage of being a frog is that you don't know you are a frog. I'm a frog but, for some weird reason, I know I'm a frog. The only way I can explain my strange condition is that I was a man in a former life and that I have come back to the world as a frog. I always thought reincarnation made no sense because people didn't remember what they had been in their former lives. Reincarnation experts tell me that it's not the person but the soul that comes back. Well, I have never been able to detect my soul. I can sense my mind, my emotions and my body, but not my soul. So I don't see how I can come back if it's just my soul that comes back. Anyway, I am not my soul, I just have a soul, I guess. If reincarnation transfers my soul and leaves behind my mind, my emotions and my body, reincarnation is not about me; it's something my soul does without me. I don't like my soul if it's going to leave me behind.

Be careful what you ask for, they say. Looks like whatever power is out there —call it the Great Reincarnator— must have decided to teach me a lesson and, apparently, he or she decided to send my mind and my emotions together with my soul on to the next reincarnation stage. Of course, knowing my luck, the next thing up for reincarnation had to be a frog. I wish it had been something more elegant, like a crane, for example. I love cranes.

So, here I am, a frog who remembers being human. I think it would have been more fun to be a man who re-members being a frog. Anyway, what else is new, things happen. Being a frog has its advantages and disad-vantages. Actually, the main disad-vantage with being a frog is the rain, or rather, the lack thereof.

I live on a flood plain. I have explored and know fairly well about two square miles of terrain. It's mostly covered with shallow water. There are some areas above water but I don't go into them much. I like the edge of the water. I like to swim a little but mostly I move around half immersed in water. I love the water.

Of course, water depends on the rain, but I also love the rain for its own sake. For a frog it's the most delightful thing on Earth. Being in the rain makes me tremble with pleasure. Each drop splashing on my skin is a source of pleasure radiating into my brain in concentric waves of pure delight; ah! skin, what a wonderful invention.

Sometimes I move about in the rain. Sometimes I just stand still, very still. Thunderstorms, showers, steady drizzle, intermittent rain, wind driven rain, vertical lazy rain, all of it soothes me. I live for the rain, I love the rain.

The problem with flood plains is that they dry out when it stops raining. It had been raining every two or three days for weeks but I knew in my heart that sooner or later it would stop. I didn't want to think about it, but I knew it would happen. The rain stopped 25 days ago. The plain has been dry for weeks.

It was okay for a while after the rain stopped. The breeze was cool and fresh and humid. I got to frolic in the mud and jump around and splash in little ponds like a kid. It was a lot of fun. Then the mud started to thicken, but it was still fun. I slid around in soft, smooth and creamy mud that looked like chocolate and smelled like the earth.

Then my frog aspects began to tell me that I couldn't stay in the surface any longer. I knew it was time to dig myself into the ground before it hardened.

Staying above without water was certain death.

I dug myself in twenty-one days ago. It was dark inside the mud. It's still dark. God! it has been dark for so long. The other frogs don't have this problem. Their bodies shut down; they go into suspended animation and they don't have to wait for the rain. My frog body does the same but, not my mind, not my emotions, not me. I have to wait for the rain. I have been waiting for the rain, here in the dark, away from the water, remembering the rain, remembering the light of the morning sun, the light of the moon after midnight, counting the days, the days, the days...

Drying out wasn't fun either. The mud dried slowly around me. I could sense the dryness creeping on down towards my head. The first thing I felt when it hit me was just a dull pain. Then it reached my back and I began to lose sensitivity all over my skin. The pain spiked at random over the steady dullness that installed itself in my body.

I remembered the rain, the grass, the fresh sensual pleasure of water surrounding me, water playing with my skin, lapping at it, kissing it; rain falling abundantly into my open mouth filling it and overflowing, ah! the rain, where's the rain? It's so dark in here.

Seven days into it, I mercifully lost all feeling in my body. I guess it finally shut down. The pain disappeared; darkness remained. Something is still active in my body. I can sense the proximity of the rain. Maybe it's just my imagination. Ten days ago a thunderstorm went by. It didn't rain though, but I knew there were clouds in the sky above me. I imagined I was a man again.

She had left ten days before. I had been missing her ever since. I was missing her like I have never missed anybody before. Missing her manifested itself physically; a dull sense of unease pervaded me at all times. I felt like a buried frog waiting for the rain. I clung to the memories I had of her and went over them over and over. It seemed that every time we had met it had been raining. I was thrilled when the rain started in late afternoon.

That evening I went to the bar we had gone together. We had talked about the ocean. I wrote her a letter that I couldn't send her. It felt good to write it anyway because I felt I could talk to her. When I left the bar, the rain was coming down in wind driven sheets. I got drenched in a few seconds. I started laughing and doing little dance steps as I went to the parking lot. I was wet down to my underwear by the time I got to my car. I went home with the windows open. The rain pelted my face as I drove through the night.

The best happened when I got home. The drain in the parking lot in front of my apartment was clogged. Water stood 8 inches deep. The wind continued to drive the rain around me. I moaned with pleasure as I walked into the shallow pool. Water flooded my shoes; cool and refreshing in my toes. I stopped and stood still for a few moments. The water lapped at my ankles kissing them. Then I went home and emptied my shoes in the sink. The wind drove the rain through the trees outside my open window as I fell asleep smiling.

Today I felt the clouds again above the ground; no rain though. Darkness and loneliness surround me in my hardened prison. I have run out of stories.

The weather front crossed onto the national park at about 4:30 AM. It was dumping rain at the rate of 3 inches per hour. At first the water didn't accumulate as the parched ground absorbed everything that came down. Then it began to pool slowly but relentlessly.

First contact was searing pain as water slid over my parched skin; then it turned quickly to pleasure and finally into an inebriating flood of sensuality. I sensed my body waking up as the dirt turned slowly to mud around me. My heart started beating faster, blood coursed through my veins and flooded each cell anew. I moved my toes. Nothing happened at first. They wiggled the third time I tried. I pushed outward with my legs. The mud caressed them as they slid around. My bones creaked. My muscles complained. My skin loved it. I began to crawl upwards. The mud hugged me. I almost fainted with pleasure when I reached the water. Then I pushed my head out of the water and into the fresh morning air. It was raining softly. Dark fresh clouds hung over the plain. A band of clear sky stretched along the eastern horizon. The light filtered through in a strange luminescence under the clouds and through the drizzle. I noticed that the underside of the clouds was turning shades of pink, yellow, and orange. I sensed the morning, I sensed the sun just below the horizon. I turned my eyes towards the light. I waited.

The crane flew overhead just as the sun rose over the horizon. I crawled out of the water. The crane flew towards the sun. Sunlight bathed me. Sunlight sank into my eyes. I felt life flooding all my body. I blinked.

I saw the plane taxiing towards the gate. I did a double take. Had I dreamed about the frog? What was I doing at the airport? I searched my memory. I drew a blank. I was obviously waiting for somebody in that plane. I began to worry. The idea of amnesia crossed my mind. Amnesia happens only in the movies. Then my reality flooded back into me suddenly and I knew I was there waiting for her. I tried to think what was all this stuff I remembered about a frog but then I saw her come out of the gate. Her face was morning light. I smiled. She smiled back and ran to me. She hugged me tight. We pulled apart. We held hands. We looked into each other's eyes. The sun peaked over the horizon and shone on our faces. It started to rain softly.

Carrboro, June 2000

THE AUTHOR

Ruy Burgos-Lovece was born in Viña del Mar, Chile, in 1957. His family moved to Venezuela when his father died in 1973. At the time, he was an exchange student in West Memphis, Arkansas. He joined his family in August that year. Eleven years later he arrived back in the US. Mr. Burgos-Lovece obtained a degree as a teacher of high school physics in 1980 in Venezuela. By 1987, he had an MA in French from the University of Arkansas at Fayetteville. He taught high school Physics and French in Fort Smith, Arkansas until 1993. By 2001, he had a PhD in French Literature from the University of North Carolina at Chapel Hill. In 1994, he started translating freelance and has been doing it assiduously ever since. In 2003, Dr. Burgos-Lovece was hired as a lecturer at UNC-CH. He currently teaches Spanish grammar, composition and translation at UNC-CH.

Tunnel Books Collection
First Series

The Frog
by Ruy Burgos-Lovece

The Woman Who Walks Backwards
by Alberto Chimal

Short the Nightmares with Alebrijes
by Carlos Labbé

In Peace
by Claudia Salazar-Jiménez

Avalanche, Diptych, and Homologous Parts
by Leila Guenther

Objectual Study of the Head
by Mónica Ríos

The Ones Who Cry
by Joel Flores

The Christ in Aucayacu
by Richard Parra